Badger's Fancy Meal

KEIKO KASZA

PUFFIN BOOKS

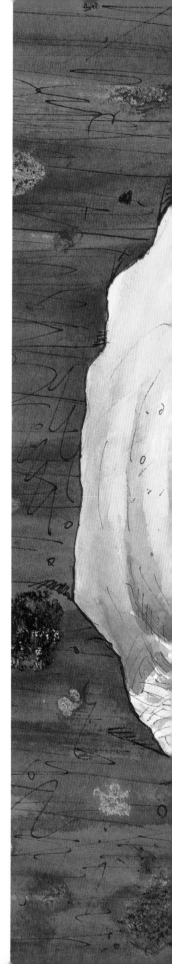

To all my friends whose suggestions
and critiques I value so much:

Elaine Alphin, Marilyn Anderson,

Patricia Batey, Joy Chaitin,

Angelene Kasza, Antonia Kasza,

Gregory Kasza, Julie Latham-Brown,

Stuart Lowry, Patricia McAlister,

Elsa Marston and Sarah Stevens.

PUFFIN BOOKS

Published by the Penguin Group

Penguin Group (USA) Inc., 375 Hudson Street, New York, NY 10014, U.S.A.

Penguin Group (Canada), 90 Eglinton Avenue East, Suite 700, Toronto, Ontario, Canada M4P 2Y3

(a division of Pearson Penguin Canada Inc.)

Penguin Books Ltd, 80 Strand, London WC2R ORL, England

Penguin Ireland, 25 St Stephen's Green, Dublin 2, Ireland

(a division of Penguin Books Ltd)

Penguin Group (Australia), 250 Camberwell Road, Camberwell, Victoria 3124, Australia

(a division of Pearson Australia Group Pty Ltd)

Penguin Books India Pvt Ltd, 11 Community Centre, Panchsheel Park,

New Delhi – 110 017, India

Penguin Group (NZ), 67 Apollo Drive, Rosedale, North Shore 0632, New Zealand

(a division of Pearson New Zealand Ltd)

Penguin Books (South Africa) (Pty) Ltd, 24 Sturdee Avenue, Rosebank, Johannesburg 2196, South Africa

Registered Offices: Penguin Books Ltd, 80 Strand, London WC2R ORL, England

First published in the United States of America by G. P. Putnam's Sons, a division of Penguin Young Readers Group, 2007

Published by Puffin Books, a division of Penguin Young Readers Group, 2009

1 3 5 7 9 10 8 6 4 2

THE LIBRARY OF CONGRESS HAS CATALOGED THE G. P. PUTNAM'S SONS EDITION AS FOLLOWS:

Kasza, Keiko.

Badger's fancy meal / Keiko Kasza.

p. cm.

Summary: Badger is bored with the same old meals, but his search for more exciting food only leads to trouble.

ISBN: 978-0-399-24603-6 (hc)

[1. Badgers—Fiction. 2. Animals—Food—Fiction.] I. Title. PZ7.K15645Bad 2007

[E]—dc22 2006008243

Puffin Books ISBN 978-0-14-241271-8

Manufactured in China

Design by Marikka Tamura

Text set in Theatre Antoine

The art was done in gouache on three-ply Bristol illustration paper.

Badger's den was full of food, but he was not happy. "Apples, worms and roots . . . same old, same old," he sighed. "I wish I could have a fancy meal for a change."

So Badger crawled out of his den and eagerly set out to find his fancy meal.

Soon Badger
spotted a mole
walking by.
"Mmm . . ." he thought. "How about
a mole taco with hot spicy salsa?
Now, that's what I call a fancy meal!"

He jumped for the mole, but it was too slippery.
It slipped and slid right out of Badger's hands.
Then it scampered away as fast as it could . . .

...and found a perfect place to hide.

Badger was
disappointed
but not for long,
because soon he spotted a rat walking by.
"Mmm-mmm . . ." he thought.
"How about a rat burger smothered
in cheese sauce? Now, that's what I call
a fancy meal."

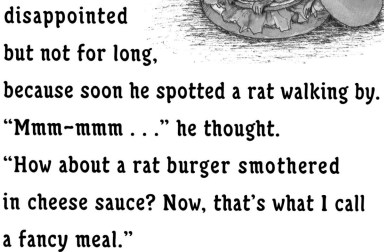

He jumped for the rat, but it was too wiggly.
It wiggled and jiggled right out of Badger's hands.
Then it scurried away as fast as it could . . .

. . . and found a perfect place to hide.

Badger was
disappointed again but
not for long, because
soon he spotted
a rabbit walking by. "Mmm-mmm-mmm . . ."
he thought. "How about a rabbit-banana split
covered with hot fudge? Now, that's what
I call a very fancy meal."

He jumped for the rabbit, but it was too quick.
It hippity-hopped right out of Badger's hands.
Then it bounced away as fast as it could . . .

. . . and found a perfect place to hide.

Poor Badger! He had lost three meals in a row.
And now he was really, really hungry. He screamed,
"I'm so hungry that I could eat a horse!"

"Oh, really?" said a loud voice.

Badger couldn't believe his bad luck. There, glaring down at him, was a big mean-looking horse.

"You? Eat me?" sneered the horse. "I don't think so."

"Now stop badgering me!" And with that, the horse kicked Badger waaaaaaaaaay up into the air.

Badger flew . . .
and flew . . .
and flew some more . . .

He landed right back where he started,
in his own den.

"Thank goodness, I made it home,"
exclaimed Badger. "Who needs a fancy
meal anyway? I have plenty of good food
right here!"

But Badger was wrong.
His food was all gone.
Instead, all he found was
a short note, which said . . .

Dear Whoever Lives Here,

Sorry for dropping by uninvited.
A nasty badger was chasing us
and we had nowhere else to hide.
The apples, worms and roots
were delicious.

Thanks for the fancy meal!

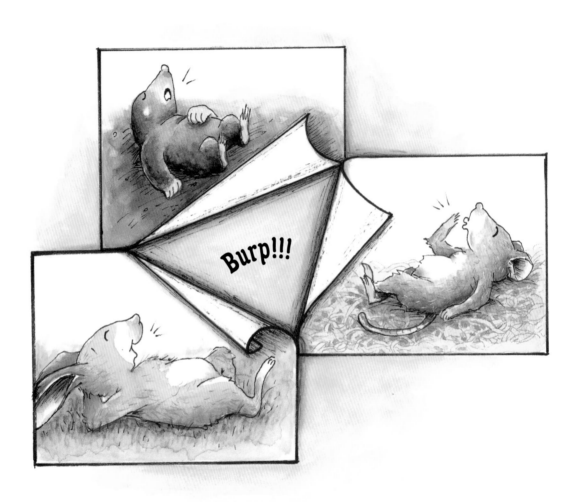

DATE DUE 2010

JUL 13 2010			
SE 10 '12			

RIDLEY PARK PUBLIC LIBRARY

107 E. Ward St.

Ridley Park, PA 19078

610-583-7207

$18.49